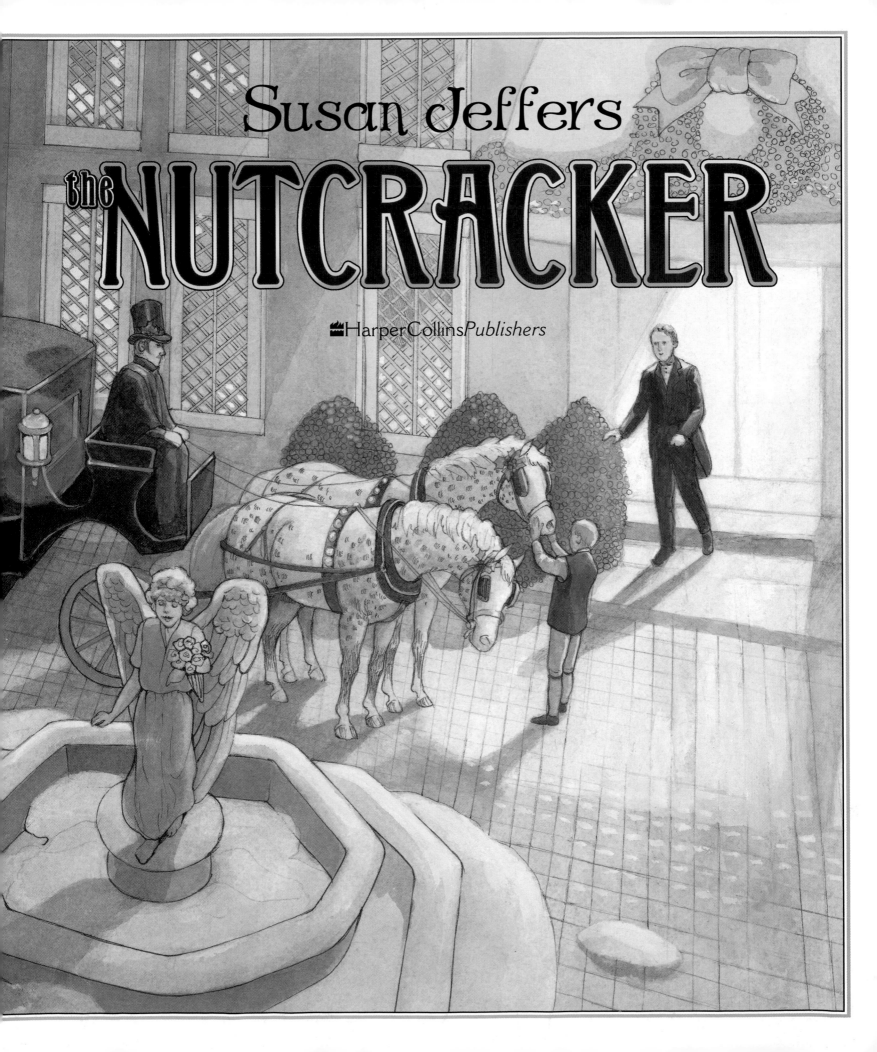

Susan Jeffers

the NUTCRACKER

HarperCollinsPublishers

It was Christmas Eve

at the Stahlbaums' house. Marie and her little brother, Fritz, were listening at the ballroom door, waiting for the party to begin.

Everyone was dancing when the last guest arrived. "Godfather!" cried
Marie, rushing back to greet him.

Herr Drosselmeier was not only Marie's godfather, but he was also a famous
toy maker. He could make toys that moved and clocks that called the hours
as sweetly as a nightingale.

Herr Drosselmeier brought presents for the children. He gave Fritz
a box of toy soldiers. For Marie, there were two dolls: Harlequin and
Columbine, who danced with each other.

"I have another present for you, Marie," said Herr Drosselmeier,
handing her a wooden Nutcracker. "I want you to take good care
of him."

"Not fair," shouted Fritz. "She has three presents."

He grabbed the Nutcracker from Marie and tossed him in the air.

The Nutcracker crashed to the floor and broke his head.

"So what," jeered Fritz. "It was an ugly thing."

Herr Drosselmeier bound Nutcracker's head with his handkerchief. Tenderly
Marie took Nutcracker into her arms. She put him under the Christmas tree.

Outside in the street, the carriages waited. After a flurry of good-byes, Fritz and Marie were sent up to bed.

But my poor Nutcracker is all alone, thought Marie, tiptoeing back downstairs. Holding Nutcracker close, she soon fell asleep.

Herr Drosselmeier slipped into the room and, raising his hand, cast a bit of magic.

Bong! Bong! Bong! The grandfather clock struck midnight. Marie stirred and rubbed her eyes. The Christmas tree was growing. Around her came a scampering of mice. *Squeak! Squeak!* They were gathering like an army to attack. Their ruler was the Mouse King, who had seven heads and seven crowns.

Marie held Nutcracker and ran as fast as she could.

Nutcracker leapt out of Marie's arms and
held his sword at the ready. Fritz's toy soldiers
took their battle positions.

Swords flashed and cannons fired. *Boom! Boom! Squeak! Squeak!*
Nutcracker fought bravely, but the Mouse King was stronger.

"No!" cried Marie. "You shall not hurt him!"

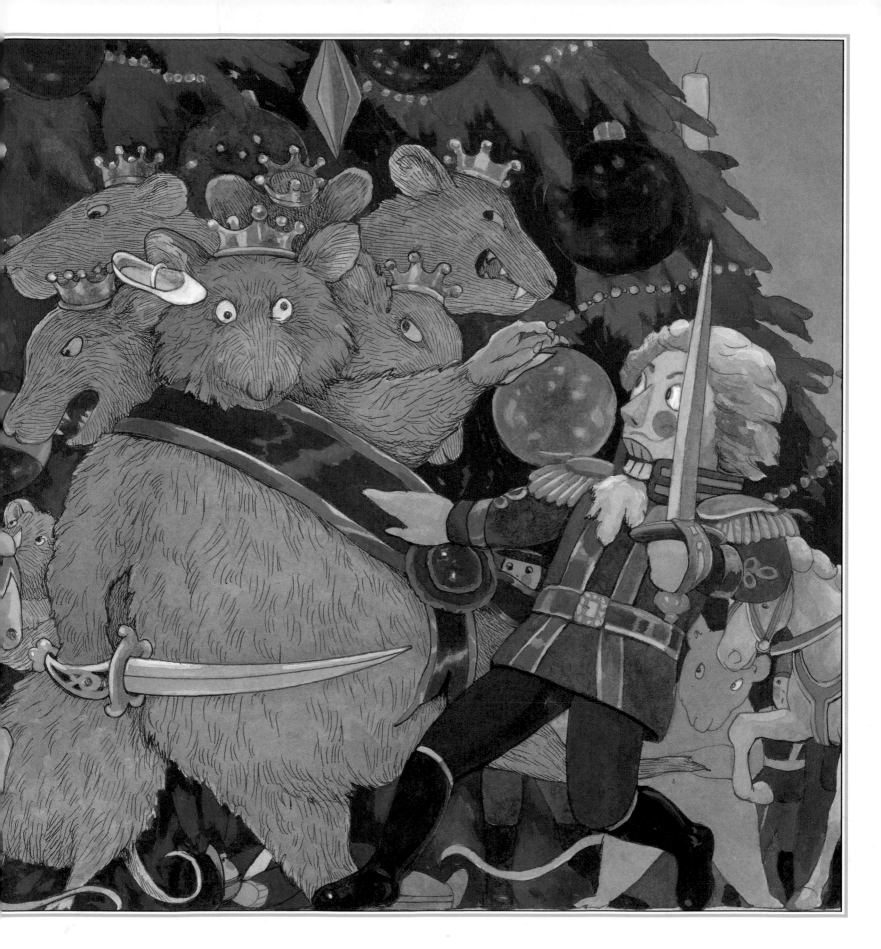

She pulled off her slipper and threw it with all her might
at the Mouse King.

With a hiss, the Mouse King sank to the floor.

Gathering up their king, the mice dragged him away.

From the shadows, Herr Drosselmeier saw Marie's bravery.

He raised his hand and Nutcracker was transformed into a handsome prince.
The Prince bowed to Marie and placed the Mouse King's sparkling crown
upon her head.

"Come," said the Prince. They walked through falling
snowflakes to a waiting boat that flew them through the night.

"Welcome to my kingdom," said the Prince.
"But where are we?" asked Marie.
"You are in the Land of Sweets," said the
Sugar Plum Fairy, coming through the gates
of the kingdom. "Welcome home, dear Prince.
We will have a party to celebrate your return."

The Sugar Plum Fairy led the Prince
and Marie to the seat of honor. Coffee,
Chocolate, Chinese Tea, Marzipan, and
Mother Ginger and her Polichinelles
danced for them.

Pink roses waltzed.
At last, the Sugar Plum Fairy danced.
She seemed lighter than air.

Too soon, it was time to leave.

As they flew homeward, Marie asked the Prince,
"Will I ever see you again?"

The Prince replied, "One day your courage and
kind heart will be rewarded. Do not forget me."

"What are you doing under the tree, Marie?" said her mother the next morning. "Wake up!" said Herr Drosselmeier. Marie opened her eyes and hugged her Nutcracker. She whispered, "If only you were alive—I would not care if Fritz said you were ugly. I would love you anyway."

Herr Drosselmeier raised his hand, and Nutcracker again became the Prince of fairyland. The Prince said to Marie, "The Mouse King imprisoned me under an evil spell. Because you love me no matter what I look like, his spell is broken. I have been returned to my true form."

Years passed and the Prince
and Marie became engaged.

After their wedding, they rode to
the Land of Sweets in a coach trimmed
in gold drawn by four silver horses.

To this day there are those who say
Marie is the Queen of a wondrous
fairyland that only those who
believe can see.

AUTHOR'S NOTE

When it was suggested that I do a book based on *The Nutcracker*, I asked myself, "Why another *Nutcracker*? Do I have something to say that hasn't already been said?" My first thought was "Maybe not." But I have long been enchanted by the ballet and wanted to see if I could contribute something new.

When I looked at all of *The Nutcracker*s available, I was struck with two things. First, they all seemed to have intricate and lengthy texts. I couldn't imagine myself reading these long retellings to a picture-book-age child.

Second, I noticed the absence of the ballet in the books available for children. My daughter danced many different roles in *The Nutcracker* during her growing-up years, and I had seen the performance every holiday season as a stage mom. My affection for *The Nutcracker* fairy tale is rooted in the ballet. Each year it delighted me; seeing it became one of my holiday traditions, as is true for countless others.

Indeed, *The Nutcracker* has been one of the most beloved ballets in the world since it was first performed in 1892 in the famous Maryinsky Theatre in St. Petersburg, Russia. E. T. A. Hoffmann's original *Nutcracker* fairy tale tells how a young man is cursed by the Mouse Queen and becomes an ugly nutcracker. Despite the way he looks, he has to win the love of a maiden before he can return to his true form. The ballet picks up the story where Marie's bravery and love save her Nutcracker.

Marie and her Nutcracker Prince sail to an enchanted kingdom, where they reign over every child's fantasy: a land of sweets. And finally the spell binding the Nutcracker is broken by the strength of Marie's devotion. It's *Beauty and the Beast*, love that sees beyond appearance. This is a theme that has no end and that we never tire of.

After attending *The Nutcracker* with my family in New York City, I decided that I had two good reasons to attempt my own version. The first was to write and illustrate a book that would follow the story of the beloved ballet, and the second was to create a book that will, I hope, speak to a child.

I'd like to especially thank Meghan Morkal-Williams for being our beautiful Marie, and Alice and Chad Phillips for their enthusiasm in playing the supporting roles and making our time in the studio such fun.

Susan Jeffers

P.S. For those who would enjoy the whole fairy tale, a full translation of the original can be found in the Lisbeth Zwerger or the Maurice Sendak version.

The Nutcracker • Copyright © 2007 by Susan Jeffers • Manufactured in China. All rights reserved • No part of this book may be used or reproduced in any manner whatsoever without written permission except in the case of brief quotations embodied in critical articles and reviews. For information address HarperCollins Children's Books, a division of HarperCollins Publishers, 1350 Avenue of the Americas, New York, NY 10019. www.harpercollinschildrens.com

Library of Congress Cataloging-in-Publication Data is available. ISBN-10: 0-06-074386-7 (trade bdg.) ISBN-13: 978-0-06-074386-4 (trade bdg.) — ISBN-10: 0-06-074387-5 (lib. bdg.) ISBN-13: 978-0-06-074387-1 (lib. bdg.). Typography by Martha Rago. 1 2 3 4 5 6 7 8 9 10 ❖ First Edition